A special thank you to Vicky McDonald for stealing my commas,
capital letters and ellipses.
You meanie!
XXX

"Amelia" Mum said, "you are going to be late for school. Come downstairs and eat your breakfast. Get dressed as quickly as you can because we still need to find your shoe."

Amelia opened one eye and yawned.

Amelia got dressed and walked downstairs. After breakfast, she set about finding her missing shoe.

She could not remember where she had left it so she asked Dad.

"Try the garage," said Dad. "I think I spotted it in there."

Amelia went to the garage to look.

Amelia couldn't see her shoe.
She did see something very tall, with sharp
edges and two giant feet at the bottom.

"What can it be?" Amelia said to herself.
"Think,think,think."
Amelia thought and thought and thought some
more and decided…

 "Dad!" Amelia shouted.
"Is there a robot in the garage?"

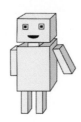

Dad came running and looked around. Then, he smiled and said **"Sometimes, Amelia, things are not as they seem. Just pull off that sheet and you'll see what I mean."**

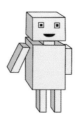

Amelia took a deep breath and bravely started pulling off the sheet.
What could be underneath if it wasn't a robot?

"Phew Dad! It's not a robot after all," said Amelia

"It's just the old washing machine, some boxes, rope and plant pots. Who would have thought?"

Dad laughed and added, "don't forget about your shoe. It's on that box there. Now, quickly put your shoes on and get your coat. Mum is waiting to walk you to school and the weather is not very nice today."

As mom and Amelia started walking Amelia noticed something very strange.

The school should be just ahead at the top of the road but it wasn't.

Amelia couldn't see her school. Instead, she saw some white clouds floating near the floor but no gate, no playground, no building whatsoever.

My school has disappeared thought Amelia. Where can it be?

"Think,think,think," she said to herself.
Amelia thought and thought and thought some
more and decided…

"Mum!" Amelia screamed.
"The school has disappeared. Has it sunk?"

Mum stood still, shocked.
After a few seconds she smiled and said.
"Sometimes Amelia, things are not as they seem. Let's walk a little further and you'll see what I mean."

Amelia took a deep breath and bravely walked forward.
If the school hadn't sunk, then where had it gone?

"Phew!" Said Amelia. "School hasn't disappeared after all. It's right here where it's always been."

Mum laughed and said, "yes, Amelia. It's still exactly where it should be. It was just hidden by the fog. Now, into class you go. Look Mrs Harris is waiting for you."

Amelia quickly went inside and sat down at her desk. Her first lesson was Art.

After Art class, Mrs Harris asked Amelia to go to the store cupboard and fetch the English books.

Amelia went to the cupboard, she looked but she couldn't see them at all.

What she did see was something pink, with long legs, feathers and a big beak.

"What is it?" Thought Amelia.
"Think, think, think."

Amelia thought and thought and thought some more and decided…

 "Mrs Harris!" Amelia called.
"Is there a flamingo in the cupboard?
Maybe it's escaped from the zoo!"

Mrs Harris looked confused as she
walked across to Amelia.
She looked in the cupboard,
smiled and said
**"sometimes Amelia, things are not
as they seem. Turn on that light and you'll
see what I mean."**

Amelia took a deep breath and bravely put an
arm into the dark cupboard to turn on the light.
If it wasn't a flamingo in there, what was it?

English

"Oh" said Amelia. "It isn't a flamingo after all. It's only an old feather duster, the megaphone from sports day and some cleaning supplies."

Mrs Harris giggled quietly and replied, "yes. Only some cleaning supplies and some shadows playing a trick on you. It's a good job really. I don't think I'd like a pet flamingo. Now, let's get on with our English lesson before lunch."

After class, Amelia joined the lunch queue.

As the lunch lady removed the lid from the tray, Amelia was very shocked. She couldn't see any food at all. She only saw something wiggly and long with big brown specks on it.

"What is that?" Thought Amelia.
"What are they trying to feed us today?"

"Think, think, think," she said aloud.
Amelia thought and thought and thought
some more and decided…

"Eurgh!" Amelia said.
"Are there worms for lunch? That is disgusting!"

So shocked that she dropped the tray lid on the floor, the lunch lady asked,
"why would I feed you worms?"
Then, she came around the counter to see what Amelia was looking at.
A few moments later, she smiled and said,
"sometimes Amelia, things are not as they seem. Wait for the steam to disappear and you'll see what I mean."

Amelia waited and waited and bravely followed her plate to the table. If there were not worms for lunch, what was there?

"Oh!" Said Amelia. "This is spaghetti bolognaise and that is so much tastier than worms."
She sat down to eat as the lunch lady returned to the kitchen shaking her head and saying, "worms for lunch, indeed!"

After lunch, Amelia enjoyed playing outside with her friends. By hometime, everyone was in quite a mess. Amelia ended up the messiest of all.

When they got home Mum said Amelia had to get straight in the bath.

When Amelia went upstairs to wash off the dirt, she saw something big and round with a blue tail and flippers in the bath.
What was it?

"Think, think, think," said Amelia.

Amelia thought and thought and thought some more and decided…

"Mum! Dad!" Amelia shouted.
"Is there a whale in the bathtub?
Did it swim up the plug hole?"

Mum and Dad came running
upstairs, looked at the bathtub
and laughed.
**"Sometimes Amelia, things are
not as they seem.
Pull back the shower curtain and you'll see
what we mean."**

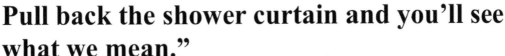

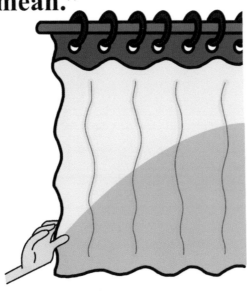

Amelia bravely grabbed the shower curtain and
began to slide it across the rail. If it wasn't a
whale behind there, what was it?

"Oh!" said Amelia.
"It isn't a whale after all. It's just some towels and a lot of bubbles."

"Yes," said Mum and Dad. "Just some bubbles. Now, into the bath to get that dirt off."

"What a day," thought Amelia as she hopped into the bubbles.

At bedtime, Amelia lay awake thinking about
all the things she had seen today.

"Some of them were very silly," she thought.
"Maybe, after I **think and think and think,** I
should **think one more time** before I call
anyone."

As Amelia rolled away from the window, she saw the strangest thing of all.
A shadow that was large and furry and had two ears.

"What can it be and how did it get up so high?" she said. **"Think, think, think."**
Amelia thought and thought and thought some more and decided…

 Amelia jumped out of bed and just as she went to yell for Mum and Dad she stopped.

 All day, she had thought she had seen one thing and it had turned out to be something else.
"Sometimes Amelia, things are not as they seem," she said to herself.

Amelia took a moment to think again.
She tiptoed over to the window and bravely reached for the curtain. She thought it still might be a bear so she closed her eyes tight and pulled.

When Amelia opened her eyes again she saw…

Amelia was very glad she did not shout for Mum and Dad. The shadow she saw was just her teddy. How silly she would have felt!

"From now on," she said, **"after I've thought and thought and thought some more…I will think again."**

She grabbed teddy, got back into bed and fell soundly to sleep.

Printed in Great Britain
by Amazon

15090023R00022